Elizabeth's Christmas Story

Luke 1:5–66 for children

Written by Vivian Hughes Dede
Illustrated by Susan Morris

Arch® Books
Copyright © 1987 Concordia Publishing House
Revised 2004
3558 S. Jefferson Avenue, St. Louis, MO 63118-3968
Manufactured in Colombia

Elizabeth is what I'm called, the wife
of Zechariah. Well along in life,
but never blessed with child. Still, my days
were full of serving God and giving praise.

Until one day—it was my husband's turn,
as priest in inner temple, there to burn
the incense as the people prayed outside—
when suddenly an angel did abide!

He said, "The Lord appreciates your prayer.
Your wife will bear a son, the Lord declares,
who will prepare the people of the earth
for God's own coming. Name him 'John' at birth."

My husband answered, "How can this be so?
We two were young so many years ago."
The angel said, "From God Himself I come!
You disbelieve! You shall be stricken dumb
until this happens." Quickly he was
gone … with Zechariah mute from that
day on.

Now I (still marv'ling that it should be so)
within me feel the blessed child grow.
Secluded, joyful, in my house I wait
when there appears a woman at my gate,
familiar, young, and pretty. Can it be …?
My cousin, Mary, comes to visit me!

"My greetings, Mary! At your welcome voice
the babe within me leaps and does rejoice.
And God gives me the wisdom to proclaim
most blest among all women is your name;
and doubly blest will be your coming child,
a Savior sent to all unreconciled.
But who am I, of such low degree,
that the mother of my Lord should come to me?"

What joy to have someone whom I could share
my story with; that she, in turn would care
to bring to me the wonder, fear, and awe
when that great messenger of God she saw!
The angel Gabriel—a perfect light—
did tell her she was favored in God's sight
and, thus, would bear a child, God's own Son.

She made reply, "God's will in me be done."
Yet how confused she was when once he
spoke those tender words of
mercy that would yoke
the name of Mary to
eternity!
To reassure her then,
he spoke of me
and how, in my old age,
I had conceived
and soon would bear a son.
So she believed.

Soon after that, upon a brilliant morn,
by God's great grace a son to us was born.
Now everyone who came assumed we call
him 'Zechariah,' though I said to all,
"Not so! He's John!" in unbelief all went
to ask the speechless father his consent
to name him Zechariah. "John!" he wrote.
He felt the healing welling in his throat—
and voice restored, he prophesied the ways
of John, his son, and sang a hymn of praise.

The winter passed before we heard the news.
A traveling merchant came to ask our views
of something he had seen in Bethlehem
at taxing time. The inn was crowded then,
and late a couple came; he, worried, old;
and she, with child great, were rudely told
to use the stable. Wakened in the night,
the merchant spoke of music, then of light.

And stepping out to stable door, he saw
rough shepherds humbly kneel upon the straw
before a manger where there lay a Child
of light most holy. Mary, meek and mild,
kept adoring watch. "What did it mean?"
the man inquired, haunted by the scene.
He must have thought us mad—or slightly
odd—as we exulting sang, "Thank God! Thank God!"

Dear Parents:

Children played an important part in the family life of Israel, both in Old Testament times and at the time of Jesus. For the Hebrew husband and wife, children were a natural consequence of marriage (Genesis 1:27–28) and considered special gifts from God (Genesis 33:5). Jewish culture viewed a marriage without children as a great misfortune, as can be seen in Luke's comments about Zechariah and Elizabeth (Luke 1:6–7).

Like Sarah and Hannah before her, Elizabeth responded to her pregnancy by praising and thanking God. " 'The Lord has done this for me ... He has shown His favor' " (Luke 1:25).

Elizabeth and Zechariah's child, John, prepared the way for God's greatest Gift to all of us: Jesus, God's own Son, our Savior. He is why the baby John leapt in Elizabeth's womb, why the angels sang that first Christmas, and why the shepherds knelt in worship at the manger bed.

Isaac, Samuel, and John were all special gifts of God's love, gifts that were loved and cherished by their parents. But the one great Gift for all time is Jesus, for through Him we ourselves are again sons and daughters of our heavenly Father, children of promise, and heirs to eternal life (Galatians 4). This is the reason we too sing with the Christmas angels and worship the promised Savior.

The Editor